Anna Grossnickle Hines

RUMBLE THUMBLE BOOM!

Greenwillow Books  New York

The full-color artwork was prepared
with colored pencils on black paper.
The text type is Horley Old Style.

Printed in Hong Kong by
South China Printing
Company (1988) Ltd.
First Edition
10 9 8 7 6 5 4 3 2 1

Library of Congress
Cataloging-in-Publication Data

Hines, Anna Grossnickle.
Rumble thumble boom! /
by Anna Grossnickle Hines.
        p.   cm.
Summary:
A child and a dog wheedle their
way under the covers with
Mommy and Daddy when the
thunder loudly booms outside.
ISBN 0-688-10911-X (trade).
ISBN 0-688-10912-8 (lib.)
[1. Thunderstorms—Fiction.
2. Bedtime—Fiction.]
I. Title.
PZ7.H572Ru   1992
[E]—dc20
91-31808   CIP   AC

To my friends at Grey Towers—including James

CRACK BAM BOOM!!

A - RUMBLE THUMBLE BOOM!!

Auntie says it's the angels rolling potatoes.
Grandpa says it's all the people in heaven
playing ninepins. He says ninepins is like
bowling, only outside.

CRACKETY RUMBLEDY BOOM!

Daddy says the lightning heats up the air, so it moves around too fast and bumps into itself. Mommy says, "That's just thunder, dear. It won't hurt you."

I say it's loud. So does my dog, Hercules. He tries
to hide underneath me, but I'm not big enough.
I try to hide under Hercules, but he's too big.

BOOM BOOM BOOM

BA-DOOOMMM M M!

Hercules whines, but I'm brave.
"Don't worry, Herc," I say. "It's just thunder.
It's just the air bumping into itself."
Herc still thinks it's scary. I do, too.
I make a cozy place for us under the bed.

RUMBLE - UMBLE

RUMBLE

GRUMBLE

DOOMM!

That old bumping air is loud. Very loud!

"Daddy's bed, Herc," I say. "He'll take care of us."

BOOM!!
BA-DA-BOOM!!
CRACKETY-CRACK!!
DOOM-KA-BLOOOMM!!

"What's this?" Daddy asks.

"It's me and Hercules," I say. "He's afraid
of the thunder."

"Oh, he is, is he? Well, crawl in." Daddy
lifts up the covers, and I snuggle in.

"Come on, Herc," I say.

"Oh, no," Mommy says. "Hercules can
sleep under the bed."

THUMBLEDY RUMBLEDY BUMBLEDY BOOOMMM!

Hercules whines.

"See?" I say. "He wants to be *on* the bed."

"All right," Mommy says. "But *not* under the covers."

RUMBLE GRUMBLE
DOOM CRACK BOOM!

"He's shaking," I say. "Feel Hercules shaking?
He *needs* to be under the covers."
"Not in *this* bed," Mommy says. "No dogs on
my sheets. Hercules is just fine where he is.
Aren't you, Herc, old boy?"
"On the sofa bed, then? Please, Daddy?
Please, Mommy? All of us on the *old* sofa
bed with the *old* sheets?"

Herc and Daddy and Mommy and I all
snuggle in. Now *that* feels cozy.

Daddy groans. Mommy shivers.

"Don't worry," I say, "It's just the air bumping into itself."